INTRODUCING TEDDY

a story about being yourself

JESSICA WALTON   illustrated by DOUGAL MacPHERSON

BLOOMSBURY

LONDON OXFORD NEW YORK NEW DELHI SYDNEY

Thank you to our wives for your support as we wrote, illustrated,
edited and promoted this book; you're both wonderful.

Thank you to Sarah Shumway, Brianne Johnson, Charlotte Walton, Tina Healy, Ally Healy,
Victoria Harrison, Erica Hateley and Jennifer Lynn for your help improving the text.

Thank you to our Kickstarter backers - we couldn't have done this without you! A special thanks
to Hamish MacPherson and family, Rob Miller, Dr Fintan Harte, East West Homes, James
Healy, Andrea Foxworthy, Ava Healy-Foxworthy, Sue Naegle, Cordelia Marie Millerwhite, Yvette
Vincent, Lynette Funnell, Charmaine Reader and Ally Healy.

Bloomsbury Publishing, London, Oxford, New York, New Delhi and Sydney

First published in the United States of America in 2016
by Bloomsbury Children's Books
1385 Broadway, New York, New York 10018

This edition first published in Great Britain in 2016 by Bloomsbury Publishing Plc
50 Bedford Square, London WC1B 3DP

A CIP catalogue record for this book is available from the British Library

ISBN 978 1 4088 7763 0 (HB)
ISBN 978 1 4088 7762 3 (PB)
ISBN 978 1 68119 211 6 (ebook)

Printed in China by Leo Paper Products, Heshan, Guangdong

1 3 5 7 9 10 8 6 4 2

www.bloomsbury.com

BLOOMSBURY is a registered trademark of Bloomsbury Publishing Plc

For my dad, Tina, and my son, Errol - I wrote this book for you; for Jeni Whelan the super librarian - your love of books was infectious; and for my brilliant, kind, hilarious friend and teacher Kate Mcirally - I miss you
J. W.

For my parents - thank you for feeding me, clothing me and providing the art supplies all those years; for my son and daughter - you give me the motivation to draw
D. M.

Errol and Thomas the teddy play together every day.

They ride their bike in the backyard.

They plant vegetables in the garden.

They have sandwiches for lunch
in the tree house.

And they have tea parties inside when it's raining.

One day, Errol woke to find the sun shining through his bedroom window.

"Hooray!" he shouted. "Come on, Thomas, let's go to the park and play!"

Thomas the teddy didn't feel like playing.

"You seem sad today, Thomas," said Errol.
"Don't worry, the park will cheer you up!"

Thomas the teddy wasn't so sure.

"Oh no, even the **swing** isn't working!
What's wrong, Thomas? Talk to me!"

"If I tell you," said Thomas, "you
might not be my friend any more."

"I will **always** be your friend, Thomas!"

Thomas the teddy took a deep breath. "I need to be myself, Errol. In my heart, I've always known that I'm a girl teddy, not a boy teddy. I wish my name was Tilly, not Thomas."

"Is that why you've been so sad?" Errol asked. "I
don't care if you're a girl teddy or a boy teddy! What
matters is that you are my friend."

"You're the best friend a bear could have," said Tilly.

"Now that you're feeling better," said Errol,
"let's call our friend Ava."

"Hi, Ava! Teddy and I are at the park. Do you want to come and play?"

"Sure, Errol! Let me just finish building my robot . . ."

"Hi, Errol! Hi, Thomas!" Ava called out as she sped towards them.

"Hi, Ava!" said Errol. "Teddy has a new name! Let me introduce you to Tilly."

"What a great name!" said Ava. "Let's go and play, Tilly!"

"Wait, I'm just moving my bow tie," said Tilly the teddy.
"I've always wanted a bow instead."

"Good for you, Tilly. Wear whatever makes you happy!" said Ava. "I think I'll get rid of my bow. I like my hair free."

Errol, Ava and Tilly
played all morning until
it was time to go home.

"See you at our next tea party," Errol said as Ava stepped on to her scooter.

"Yes, see you there. I'm bringing a friend!" Ava yelled as she sped away.

Errol and Tilly the teddy play together every day.

They ride their bike in the backyard.

They plant vegetables in the garden.

They have sandwiches for lunch
in the tree house.

And they have tea parties inside when it's raining.

Tilly